First published in Great Britain in 2003 by Brimax™,
A division of Autumn Publishing Limited
Appledram Barns, Chichester PO20 7EQ

Text and illustrations copyright © Autumn Publishing Limited 2003

Mc Graw Hill **Children's Publishing**

This edition published in the United States of America in 2003 by
Gingham Dog Press
an imprint of McGraw-Hill Children's Publishing,
a Division of The McGraw-Hill Companies
8787 Orion Place
Columbus, Ohio 43240-4027

www.MHKids.com

Library of Congress Cataloging-in-Publication Data is on file with the publisher.

Printed in China.

1-57768-482-6 (HC)   1-57768-931-3 (PB)

1 2 3 4 5 6 7 8 9 10 BRI 09 08 07 06 05 04 03

Schooltime for Sammy

By
Lynne Gibbs

Illustrated by
Melanie Mitchell

Columbus, Ohio

While his brother and sister got ready for the first day of school, Sammy played. He climbed his favorite tree and swung from branch to branch.

His brother, Fred, pushed books into his school bag and called up, "You're old enough to go to school this year, Sammy."

"I don't want to go to school. I want to stay home and play," replied Sammy.

"But school is fun, and you'll learn all kinds of things," said Sammy's sister, Sophie.

"I'm not going!" said Sammy, dangling upside down and making a face. "I already know everything. I know how to climb the tallest trees and I can swing really fast. So there! Catch me if you can!"

But Fred and Sophie didn't chase after him—they didn't want to be late for school.

Sammy spent the morning playing but soon got bored.

"What's wrong, Sammy?" asked his mom, when she found him moping.

"There's nobody to play with," grumbled Sammy.

"Well, all your friends are at school," said his mom. "Maybe you should go, too."

"No way!" shouted Sammy, scrambling back up the tree.

At last, Sophie and Fred returned home, chattering excitedly about their busy day. Sammy ran to greet them with some bananas.

Sammy wanted Fred and Sophie to play with him, but they said that they had homework to do. Sammy did not want to be left out.

"I can do homework," he said, climbing onto a chair and joining them at the table.

"How many days are there in April?" Fred asked Sophie.

"Twenty-five ninety zillion!" shouted Sammy, trying to help.

"Oh, Sammy, don't be silly. We're trying to work," said Sophie.

When Sammy's friend Jack came to visit, he was full of news about his new school.

"The teacher is really nice, and I've learned lots of important things," said Jack proudly. "I know what two plus one plus two is."

"So do I!" said Sammy, trying to count on his fingers.

"What is it then?" asked Jack.

"It's, um, it's . . . a lot!" he answered.

"You don't know!" said Jack.

"I even learned how to write my own name," Jack continued. He picked up a stick and carefully wrote J-A-C-K in the dirt.

"I can write my name too. Look!" said Sammy.
"That's not writing, that's just a scribble," said Jack.

Now Sammy was curious about school.
"What else did you do at school?" he asked.
"Well, I made lots of new friends and we all played games together," said Jack.

As Sammy listened, Jack told him everything that he had learned. His favorite part of the day was Show and Tell, when kids could bring in special things and share them with the class.
"You really did do a lot," said Sammy with a sigh.

"I'll paint you a picture of a tree, if you want," offered Jack, to cheer up his friend. "That's another thing I learned today!"

Hardly blinking, in case he missed anything, Sammy watched as Jack brushed paints over a piece of paper.

"That's the best picture in the whole world!" said Sammy.

When Jack had gone, Sammy tried to draw a tree himself, but his painting looked like a messy blob.

That night at supper, Sammy was very quiet. He did not even feel like eating his dinner. Nobody noticed, though, because Sophie and Fred were chattering loudly about school.

"I got a gold star on my spelling test," bragged Sophie.

"I won a race at recess," said Fred proudly.

"Well done, both of you," said their mom and dad.

After supper, Sammy decided that he wanted to be as smart as his brother and sister. Very quietly, he crept over to Sophie's school bag and slipped out a book. Sitting in a corner, he opened the book and tried to read it. But it was no use—the words just looked like squiggles to him.

When Sophie and Fred found Sammy with the book, they read him the story. It was a thrilling tale about pirates.

The next morning, Sammy woke up early. He was very excited as he searched for the little school bag that his mom had made for him. When he found it, he packed Effalump, his favorite toy, carefully inside. He wanted to have something for Show and Tell.

Sammy marched into the kitchen and announced, "I'm ready!"

Sammy's family looked up in surprise.

"Ready for what, Sammy?" asked his dad.

"I want to go to school after all," declared Sammy. "I want to learn how to read and write and count and draw beautiful pictures."

"That's wonderful," said his mom. "But first you'll need to have some breakfast."

After breakfast, Sammy set off with Sophie and Fred, walking fast.

"I'm already a day late for school," said Sammy with a grin. "I don't want to miss any more!"